To Andrea Kale Marcus, the girl next door

— C F

To my parents for their endless support,
to Ben for holding chairs in various positions
and to family and friends for their
constant encouragement

— M K

Tundra Books, a division of Random House of Canada Limited,
a Penguin Random House Company

Library and Archives Canada Cataloguing in Publication

Fagan, Cary, author
        Little blue chair / Cary Fagan ; illustrated by Madeline Kloepper.

Issued in print and electronic formats.
ISBN 978-1-77049-755-9 (bound).—ISBN 978-1-77049-757-3 (epub)

        I. Kloepper, Madeline, illustrator II. Title.

PS8561.A375L59 2017   jC813'.54   C2015-904002-7
                                                C2015-904003-5

Published simultaneously in the United States of America by Tundra Books
of Northern New York, a division of Random House of Canada Limited,
a Penguin Random House Company

Library of Congress Control Number: 2016933018

Edited by Tara Walker and Jessica Burgess
Designed by Rachel Cooper
The artwork in this book was rendered in ink and pencil and finished digitally.
The text was set in Tribute.
Printed and bound in China

www.penguinrandomhouse.ca

1 2 3 4 5   21 20 19 18 17

Little Blue Chair

words by Cary Fagan

pictures by Madeline Kloepper

TUNDRA BOOKS

Boo had a favorite chair.

It was little.

It was blue.

He liked to sit on it while he ate his breakfast

and his lunch

and his dinner.

He carried it outside and

sat among the daffodils looking at books.

He made a tent around it.

He fell asleep on it.

And then Boo grew bigger.

He grew too big for the little blue chair.

So his mom put it at the end of the lawn.

She made a sign and hung it on the chair.

The sign said, PLEASE TAKE ME.

A truck came rattling by.

It stopped.

A man got out and put the chair in the back of the truck.

The man sold it to a lady who ran a junk shop.

It stayed in the shop for a long time.

One day a woman came in.

The chair will be perfect, she thought.

The woman put the chair by the window.

On the chair, she put a pot with a little plant in it.

She watered the plant.

It grew.   And grew.   And grew.

The plant grew into a tree. The woman dug a big hole in her garden for it.

She didn't need the little blue chair anymore.

So she put it at the side of the road and hung a sign on it.

The sign said, FREE TO A GOOD HOME.

A boat's captain strolled by on his way to the harbor.
He saw the chair.

It will be perfect, he thought,
and he carried it on his shoulder.

On the boat, he put it beside the captain's wheel.

Now his daughter could sit beside him while they sailed across the ocean.

At last the boat reached shore.
The captain decided it was time for
them to stay in one place, so he turned
the boat into a snug little house.

They didn't need the little blue chair anymore so the captain put it on the beach with a sign that said, DO YOU NEED THIS?

The chair stood on the beach for a long time.

One day a man and an elephant walked along the beach.

The man looked at the little blue chair.

It will be perfect, he thought.

The man politely asked the elephant to kneel down.

He put the little blue chair on the elephant's back.

They walked along while the man called out, "Elephant rides! Elephant rides!"

Children lined up for a ride on the elephant.

The elephant was very gentle.

After a few years, the man and the elephant decided to retire. They didn't need the chair anymore so the man wrapped it up in brown paper, stuck a lot of stamps on it and put it in the mail to his sister.

The sister found the package on her doorstep.

She opened the package and saw the little blue chair.

It will be perfect, she thought.

She put a bowl of seeds on the chair.
Then she used a rope to raise the
chair to the top of a tree.

From all around, birds appeared in the air.
Little birds, big birds, plain birds and fancy birds —
they all perched on the chair to eat the seeds.

"How lovely," said the sister.

Some of the seeds fell to the ground.

They grew into a beautiful garden.

Now the birds spent all their time

feeding in the garden.

The sister didn't need the little blue chair anymore.

So she put the chair out with a sign on it that said, I LIKE TO WORK.

A few moments later, a carnival owner
came by and saw the chair.

It will be perfect, he thought.

The carnival had a big Ferris wheel.

But the Ferris wheel was missing one seat.

The man installed the little blue chair.

Up, up it went! Round, round it went!
The children screamed with pleasure.

After a few years, the motor on the Ferris wheel wore out.
So the carnival owner decided to dismantle it and
use all the pieces to build a copy of the Eiffel Tower.

(The copy of the Eiffel Tower was very popular.)

The man didn't need the little blue chair anymore.

So he got an old can of paint and turned the little blue chair red.

Then he used it as a prize in a contest.

Whoever could throw a ring around a milk bottle would win the chair.

Many people tried. At last a boy threw the ring.

It zipped through the air and fell over the milk bottle.

The winner!

The boy took the little chair home.

He thought of all kinds of things to use it for.

He built a go-kart and used the
chair as the driver's seat.

He wrote a play about a king and
used the chair as the king's throne.

He got a bunch of balloons and tied them to the chair.

The boy wanted the balloons to carry him into the sky.
But before he could sit down, the balloons lifted
the chair away.

"Hey, come back!" the boy called.

But balloons don't listen to people.

The chair floated back over the ocean.

It floated over towns and cities

and schools and playgrounds.

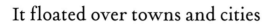

The balloons began to come down.

The little chair landed in a front garden,

right among the daffodils.

A man came out of the house. He looked at the chair.

The red paint had chipped and he could see blue underneath.

"You look familiar," said the man,

whose name was Boo.

Sure enough, he was the same boy who had loved the chair a long time ago, only now he was grown up.

One leg had become wobbly. So the man took it into the garage.

He glued the chair's wobbly leg.

He gave it a new coat of blue paint.

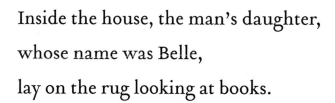

Inside the house, the man's daughter,
whose name was Belle,
lay on the rug looking at books.

"Here's a chair for you,"
said her father.

Belle carried the chair to the corner.

She put a pile of books beside it,

and also a glass of milk and a plate of cookies.

She sat on the chair.

She smiled.

"This chair is perfect," she said.